I0784004

Fantabulous Universe

Fantabulous Universe

Jan Van Ryckeghem

SilverWood

Published in 2018 by SilverWood Books

SilverWood Books Ltd
14 Small Street, Bristol, BS1 1DE, United Kingdom
www.silverwoodbooks.co.uk

ISBN 978-1-78132-776-0 (hardback)

British Library Cataloguing in Publication Data
A CIP catalogue record for this book is available
from the British Library

Pages designed and typeset according to
the author's creative direction

Printed on responsibly sourced paper

Contents

Prologue   9
Mr Cantbebuthappy   10
Happy the Left-legged Centipede   12
Deep-sea Flicksh   14
Horny Hen   16
Trippy Cat   18
Billy Bullseyes   20
Ellie the Piggyrhino   22
Drabby Dog   24
Punch the Kickboxer   26
Heady Horse   28
The Lovers   30
Huffy the Slogdog   32
Theophilus Tortoise   34
Louis the Marquis of Paradis   36

Spacey Piggy 38
Cosy Cow 40
Equus the Fisherman 42
Ollie with the Thousand Eyes 44
Emcee Hop 46
Clark the Lady-killer Sponge 48
Rocinante 50
Carrot the Rabbit 52
Lily Lamb 54
Lakey the Swan 56
Thea Turkey 58
Dody Dog 60
Belle the Canto-kitten 62
Oozy the Lovebug 64
Epilogue 67
About the Author 69

Prologue

Fate has brought you to this page,
Dear reader, let us now assuage
Your apprehension and unease.
All concerns we will appease,

Presenting marvels of creation –
A fantabulous population
From a seemingly distant universe
Eagerly will engage in verse

And share with you its dreams and foibles.
You will hear a range of voices
Whisper gently in your ears.
Trust they're real, and drop your fears.

Join us in our conversations.
Share our wildest aspirations.
Perhaps you'll even realise
That some of us you recognise…?

To find out more just turn this page.
We're waiting for you on our stage –
We, Fantabunals, so diverse
In our Fantabulous Universe!

Howdy? *Hola*! How d'you do?
Delighted to run into you!
Pleased to meet you I dare say,
On such a lovely, sunny day!

I can't help but laugh and shine,
It's a natural style of mine.
And whichever way I go,
I have to tip my chapeau,

Say 'Hi,' 'Hello', 'Bonjour!'
If you're aloof, I am the cure!
Is your appearance too austere?
I'll crack your armour with my cheer.

For I am love and share my heart
With those of you who are taken apart
By life's troubles, and pain.
I'll make you laugh, and joy will reign.

Cantbebuthappy is my name.
Making you sparkle is my aim.
I serve love by the kilogram.
It's what I do, it's who I am.

Mr Cantbebuthappy

Breezing through life in utter bliss
I leap across every abyss,
While in constant adoration
Of the wonders of creation!

Life is light, and food is fun.
Come, the party has just begun!
I can't wait to drink and dance,
Flirt and chat up and romance!

At the slightest hint of pleasure
I dive in. I know no measure!
Head on, full speed, racing fast,
Pedal to the metal, it's a blast!

All the hearts of men I capture
With my sheer delight and rapture!
I just press them to my breast
In a never-ending fest.

At any time I go for broke.
I do my nails; it is no joke:
Five hundred of them, one by one,
I don't stop until they're done.

Then I resume with steady pace
My life of overwhelming grace.
Some people say I am distorted,
But at all times, I'm supported.

I am sustained, day and night,
Can never fall, that makes life bright.
My name is Happy. It's my creed.
I'm a left-legged centipede.

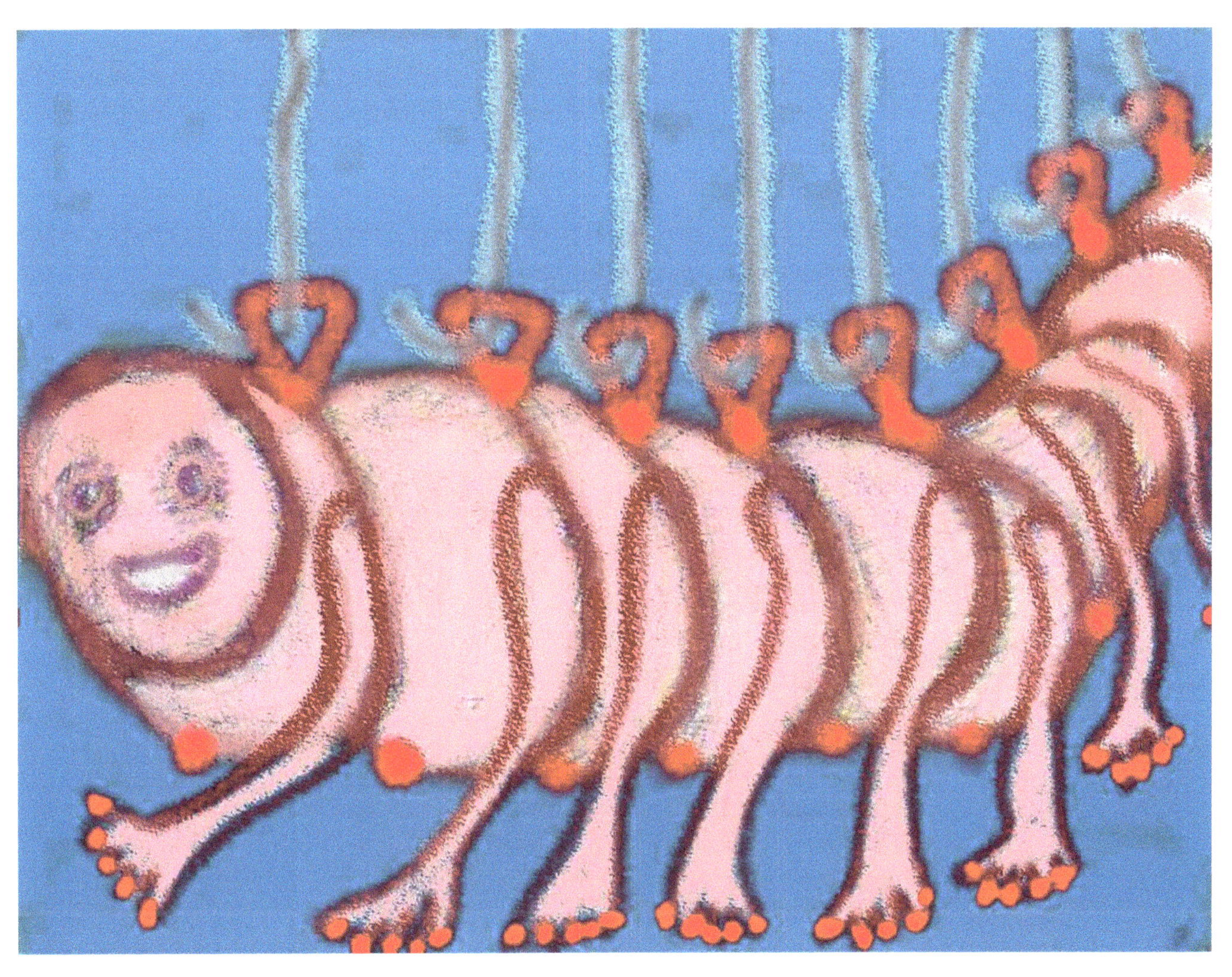

Happy the Left-legged Centipede

The brightest fish you've ever seen,
   I'm yellow, brown and blue and green.
Born in the darkness of the deep,
I cross the oceans, never sleep.

You'll find that I am far from frail.
All my strength is in my tail.
It makes me mighty as a bear,
Just like Samson and his hair.

Wish for it, and I can fly
From deepest sea to mountain high.
My tail propels me through the air.
The birds look up in sheer despair.

Like a dancer high on samba,
Rumba, mambo and marimba,
When I shake my glorious hips,
All planets align in an ellipse.

All the stars are with me, dancing.
Rhythm is just so entrancing.
All you guys and all you chicks,
Join in and swing with Deep-sea Flicksh!

Deep-sea Flicksh

Every minute I'm on fire
With continuous desire.
I just can't help my craving,
But no worries, I'm behaving!

What you see is what I am;
I'm a flammable madame.
I so savour carnal contact
'Cause I'm horny; that's a fact.

Apart from being so excited,
I'm a little bit near-sighted,
So I need a pair of specs
To spot and lure the other sex.

Libido is my middle name,
Admittedly, I have no shame.
I'm hot. What can I say?
I just love rolling in the hay.

My lust you'll never ration;
I'm a pinnacle of passion,
Always yearning to seduce
A rooster, swan or goose.

All poultry is fair game,
I like them all; they're all the same!
Watch out, women! Look out, men!
Here I come. I'm Horny Hen!

Horny Hen

You caught my eye and in one glance
You put me in a chronic trance.
All bewitched and beguiled.
My brain zonked out, my eyes turned wild.

The look of you is mesmerising.
It's got me wildly fantasising,
Leaving me floored, breathlessly
Filled with rapture and ecstasy.

My paws turn into royal jelly,
I sink straight down onto my belly,
Will only rise at your command
To travel to the Promised Land.

For a moment, time is frozen,
All my cells are decomposing,
Turning into colours bright
And fields of incandescent light.

Everything is and is not,
And with harmonious chaos fraught.
I am the future. I am history,
United with God's mystery.

How every atom's filled with sense!
Description fails; it's too immense!
Afflicted with the sweetest curse,
I'm a trippy cat in the Universe!

Trippy Cat

A paragon of scorn and fright,
The sight of me inspires flight,
'A monstrous, hideous aberration!'
'Disturbed distortion of creation!'

All these names I have been called,
For all who see me are appalled
By my head - its sheer size,
And my second pair of eyes!

Where I show up, all disappear;
The way I look is just too queer.
They express their total rejection
By bolting off in any direction.

They shouldn't run because sincerely
I can't even view them clearly.
I have four eyes but cannot see
Farther than an inch or three.

So here I stand, once more alone.
I'm used to it, don't want to moan,
But can't hide that it's disconcerting,
And my tender heart is hurting.

All I want, I'm trying to say,
Is some friends so I can play,
Just like all the other kids,
And be accepted in their midst.

I won't give up, I've learned to cope.
I'm persevering, and I hope
That one day all this pain will end
And I'll be blessed with many a friend!

Billy Bullseyes

Not so long ago, I was born
   With two legs and a horn…
Or a trunk? I don't know!
But what *is* sure is that I glow.

I'm kind of fluorescent
With a glow so incandescent
That as soon as I left the womb
I was lighting up the room.

All turned happy and, oh boy,
My folks were brimming with pure joy!
Dad stopped all his nervous pacing,
Started kissing and embracing.

So be assured, I can allege
That I will soften the roughest edge.
And all of you who like to brood,
I'll brighten up your darkest mood.

My name is Ellie, and if I may
There's one more thing I'd like to say.
Teaching is my deep desire –
To instruct and to inspire!

Though I've never gone to college
I can't wait to share my knowledge,
Writing with chalk on the board,
No pupil would ever be bored.

To close, I must confess one vice;
I just love to be precise.
So though I may look quite romantic,
I am, in fact, a bit pedantic!

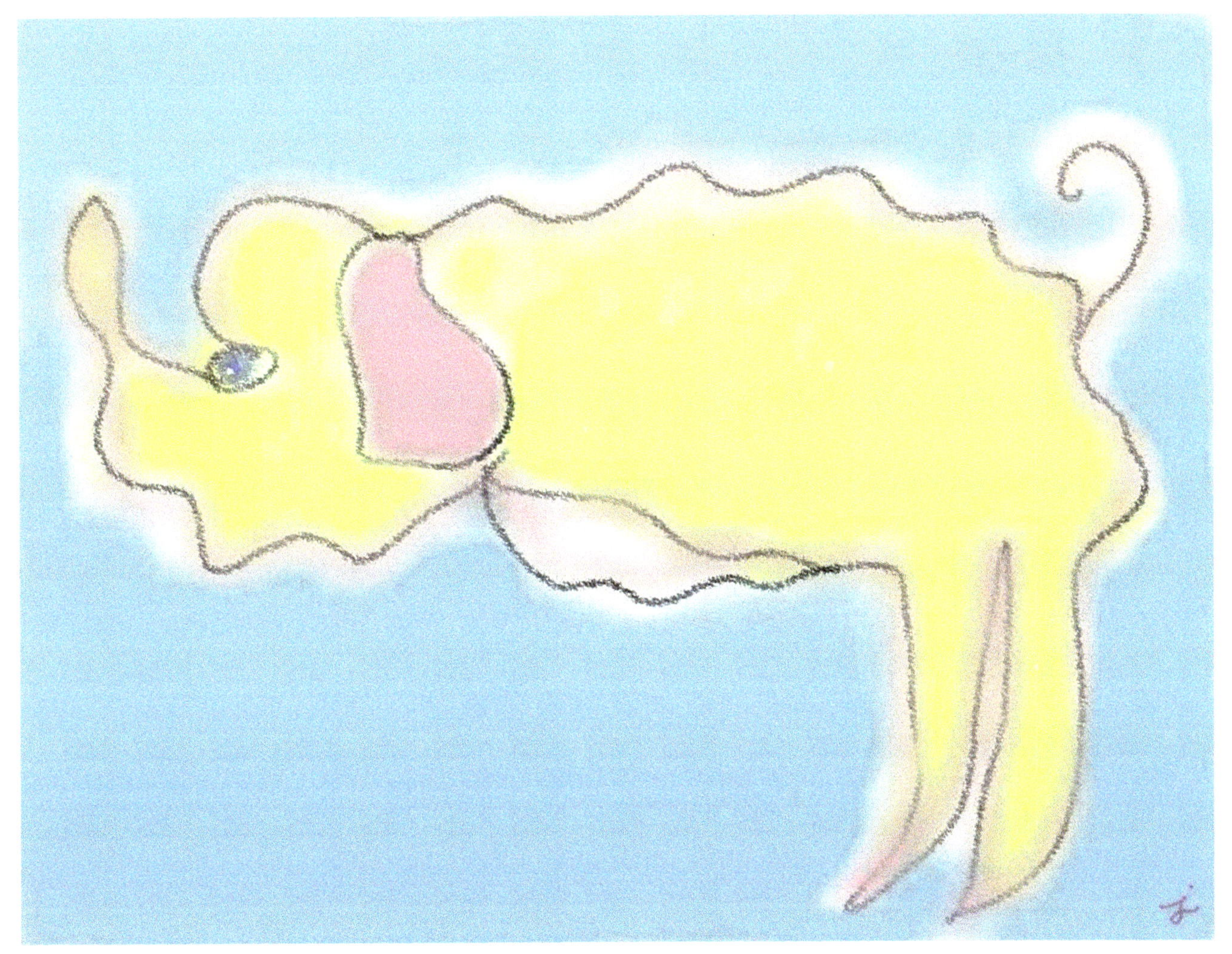

Ellie the Piggyrhino

I don't know much. What to say?
Life seems to me a little grey,
Confusing, puzzling and unclear,
Mixed with worry, angst and fear.

No one ever asks my opinion.
Guess I was trained to be a minion,
A lackey, a flunky or not even that.
With every task, I just fall flat.

I don't excel at anything.
My life is just one big downswing.
No red carpet, only bumps,
It's like I'm in an eternal slump.

I try my best but don't succeed,
Never attempt to take the lead,
But always end up at the back,
Hiding from the next attack.

I'm sorry to take up so much space;
I don't deserve to be on this page.
My grave affliction is so severe
That all I want is to disappear.

I have two mouths, but when I speak,
All of my words are weak and bleak.
I am a dog. My name is Drabby.
Can't help it, but my life is shabby.

Drabby Dog

I am the master of the ring.
   Of my prowess the bards do sing.
My foes have given up their hopes
'Cause they're hanging on the ropes.

My attitude is just as brash
As my wild and fierce moustache,
For I'm a boxer! Flat is my nose!
Yet this whole show is just a pose.

There is too much in life I miss
So I seek a different type of bliss,
Another kind of satisfaction -
Guilty pleasures, secret actions.

I love polishing my boots;
If I'd a torso, I'd wear suits.
Don't leave the house without mascara.
If I could, I'd wear a tiara.

I comb my hair, tied in a bow
When to Sunday Mass I go
And humbly kneel in the pew
Praying for all I'd love to do.

Oh, I would love to be a priest,
To celebrate Mass, that sacred feast,
Or a bishop with a staff and mitre…
Then my heart would be so much lighter!

But alas, I have no arms.
Can just enchant you with my charms.
I am soft, and I am sweet,
The cutest guy you'll ever meet.

They call me Punch. I am a fighter,
Always hoping life will get brighter!
To lively colours, I toast and drink,
And my favourite - fluorescent pink!

Punch the Kickboxer

To start, I'd like to make myself clear.
  I don't quite know how I ended up here.
It is not exactly as if I'm lost
Or can't recall which rivers I've crossed,

Roads I've walked or oceans I've sailed.
It's not like my memory has failed.
It's more that I feel so undefined,
And all my strength is left behind.

It feels like I'm wandering in a haze,
Drifting about in a mounting daze,
Like a mist of memories of ancient times
Is seeping through my mind's confines.

I must admit I'm perplexed and blue
From living in this endless hue.
Pretty it is, but I don't know where I am,
Like someone has scrambled my inner programme.

I hopelessly try to find an estimation
Of the meaning of my life, an approximation.
My name is Heady. I am a horse.
And I can't help feeling that I'm desperately off course.

Heady Horse

'Who are you? Please stop walking.
Join me for a bit of talking.
Oh, sweet nothings, not much more,
Anything that you adore.'

'Well, look at that, and who are you?
I just felt a little blue,
Pondered life and dragged my feet.
Now you appear and want to meet!'

'I just felt we had to chat,
Share some thoughts on this and that,
Assemble of our lives the puzzle,
And in between, maybe, a nuzzle?'

'Oh, yes, please! Come nearer!
Having you close makes you feel dearer.
To me, you truly are a treasure
Which fills me with abundant pleasure.'

'I just love the way you look,
The perfect picture in my book.
Don't dare to say, but yes, it seems
That you're the woman of my dreams.'

'Oh, you're too sweet. I love you so!
Feel how our bodies are aglow.
Let's stare into each other's eyes
And see stars twinkle in their skies.'

The Lovers

nger is my middle name.
I let it out; I know no shame.
I bark, bellow, and howl.
Feel something's wrong if I don't yowl!

I feel the urge and must be loud,
Don't feel good if I don't shout.
When I feel wronged (that's all the time),
I instantly expose the crime

Of anyone who's been unkind.
I tell you, I must speak my mind
And let him know I don't feel fine;
That her behaviour's out of line.

In my rage, I give 'em loads.
My eyes pop out, my head explodes!
My blood is boiling at full heat;
I tear at them 'til they're mincemeat.

My name is Huffy. How do you do?
I'm a slogdog; grunt on cue.
I wallow in this endless wrath.
It is my way; it is my path.

Huffy the Slogdog

Lazing about in the sun
Is my idea of having fun.
It's just so good in the here and now;
I'll stay a bit longer enjoying the Tao.

I'm Theophilus Tortoise. How do you do?
The oldest animal in this zoo.
So to speak, I am older than God
And I can't be moved by poke or prod.

When I was born, I don't recall.
I either lie at rest, or crawl.
To look at the world I sometimes sneak
From under my shell and take a peek.

But don't be fooled. I'm a paradox.
I beat a hare in a race…or was it a fox?
Whatever it was, it led to the conclusion
That all motion is just an illusion.

So I am the one who sees through it all,
The secrets of life, great and small.
Everyone says that I am slow,
But I eternally go with the flow.

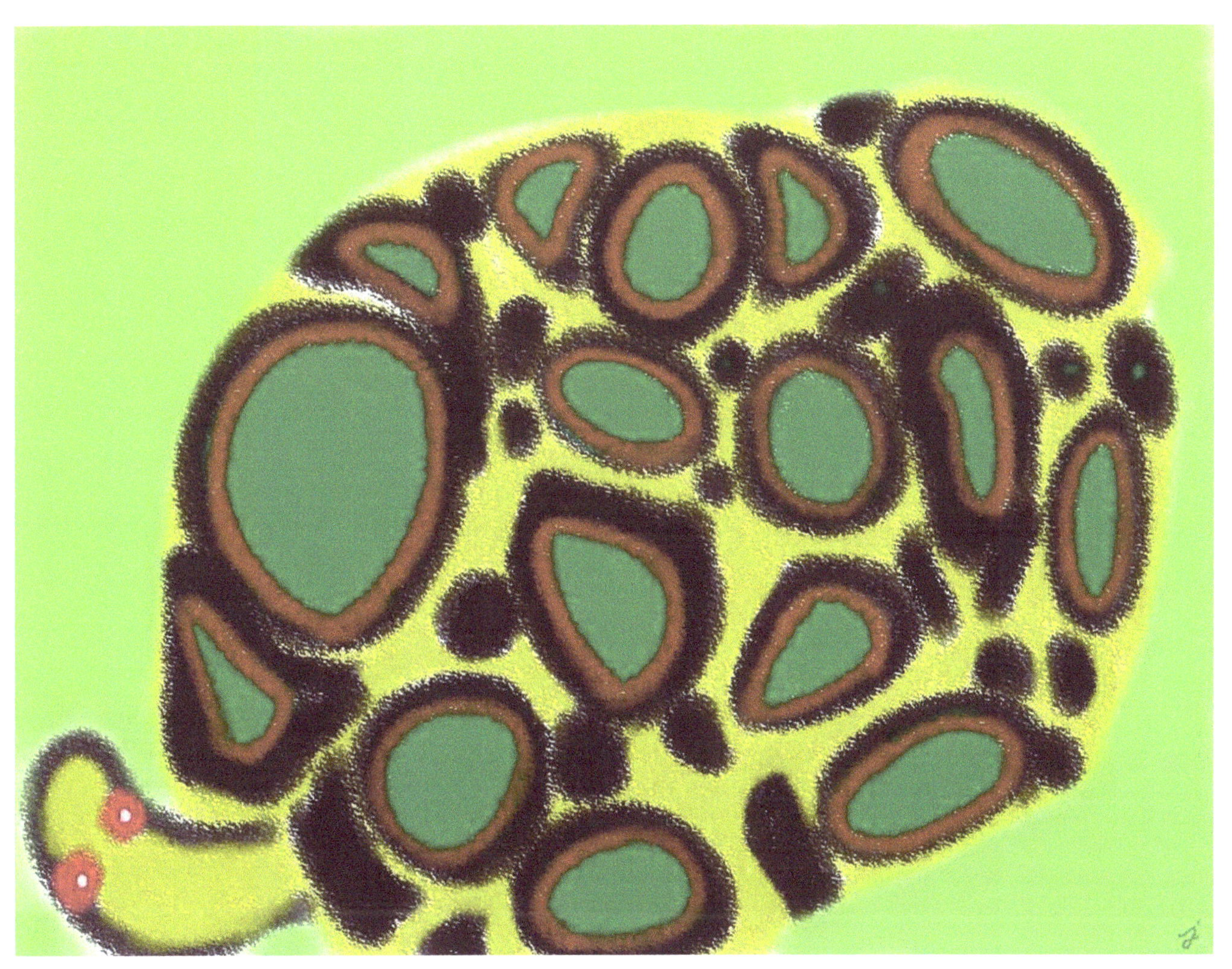

Theophilus Tortoise

Listen up, you all, take heed.
You are looking at a different breed.
To you, I may seem like a ghoul,
But I am the epitome of cool!

I am suave, urbane, sophisticated,
By every jealous husband hated.
One look at me and you'll agree,
Women throw themselves at me!

Stop staring! I will not repeat!
If you cannot control that need,
Without giving any pause
I will grab you with my claws

And will not listen to your plea
But readily toss you into the sea.
Start muscling up your every limb;
For you will surely have to swim.

I roll my fags; I love to smoke,
But I am not your average bloke.
Your name's Joe. Mine is Louis;
I am the Marquis of Paradis!

Louis the Marquis of Paradis

Floating around in your head,
Words and wishes left unsaid.
Being adrift in deepest space,
Then vanishing without a trace.

Reappearing in a flash!
Gone again with a dash.
Now I'm here; then I'm there,
Nowhere at all and everywhere.

Watching you with wistful eyes,
Sadder than the greyest skies.
Don't be afraid; it's what I do:
Begging for love and feeling blue.

It's my aim, and it's my mission.
Heartache is my ammunition.
I'm Spacey Piggy; I feel blue
And keep your heart forever in view.

Spacey Piggy

Daily, I grazed in the meadow,
Gazing around, feeling the flow,
Munching grass and chasing flies
With my tail. My exercise.

All was pleasant and serene,
The pastures tranquil, grass green.
Never thought this could be changed,
Or my life would become deranged.

Then one dawn, it all was gone
Within the timespan of a yawn,
All of life had turned to ice.
I can't describe this strangest of sights!

All of creation had suddenly frozen;
People and nature stopped in motion.
I thought I was dreaming, it was all so weird.
The world I knew had disappeared!

Didn't know where on earth I was,
Couldn't moo, felt at a loss.
Wanted to run…was gliding,
Tried not to fall…kept sliding.

Came to a stop right on this spot
And caught my balance on this dot.
Now I feel stuck in this place,
Pondering my fall from grace.

They used to call me Cosy Cow,
But I am caught in the here and now,
And I don't know just how I feel,
How to get out, or what's the deal.

The only comfort that remains
Helps me survive these chilling plains:
I stand here on these icy blocks
Because of Grandma's woollen socks!

Cosy Cow

I am a horse, born with wings.
  I feel the wind; it softly sings.
Up here, above, high in the sky,
Like an angel, I can fly.

I am of an ethereal disposition –
Legendary superstition –
Like a ghost, showing up at night,
Rising as heaven's satellite.

Silently, I supervise
The world asleep, down from the skies.
Tune into never-ending streams
Of sleeping people and their dreams.

I patiently hang out and wait,
Hook on line, no need for bait.
What do I catch? What is my goal?
It is the sparkles of the soul.

When the sombre night is ending
And in the east the sun's ascending,
About to set the world ablaze,
I throw my catch into its rays.

So it happens that this essence
Returns to people and their existence.
It is through the light of day
This glistering dust discovers its way

Into the eyes and hearts of men,
Refuelling their lives all over again.
This is my story. My name, your wish?
It is Equus, and I fish.

Equus the Fisherman

Furtively, I'm on the run
From all the things that I have done.
I wish I could tell you why
I'm convinced I have to fly.

I'm in a hurry. Can't you see
My super-urgent need to flee?
I tell you, it is me they're after,
And I can't run any faster.

If they catch me what shall I do?
Honestly, I have no clue
What would happen in the event
That I can't dodge all this torment.

I have to run, I cannot hide.
Can't do more, my hands are tied;
Can't say more, my lips are sealed
So much that they feel congealed.

My name is Ollie and I have eyes,
A thousand of them; they're my spies,
Looking out for me. They're my salvation
And help me with my preservation.

I trust that you can comprehend
That I don't know where this will end.
I keep running as if I'm late.
Perhaps paranoia is just my fate!

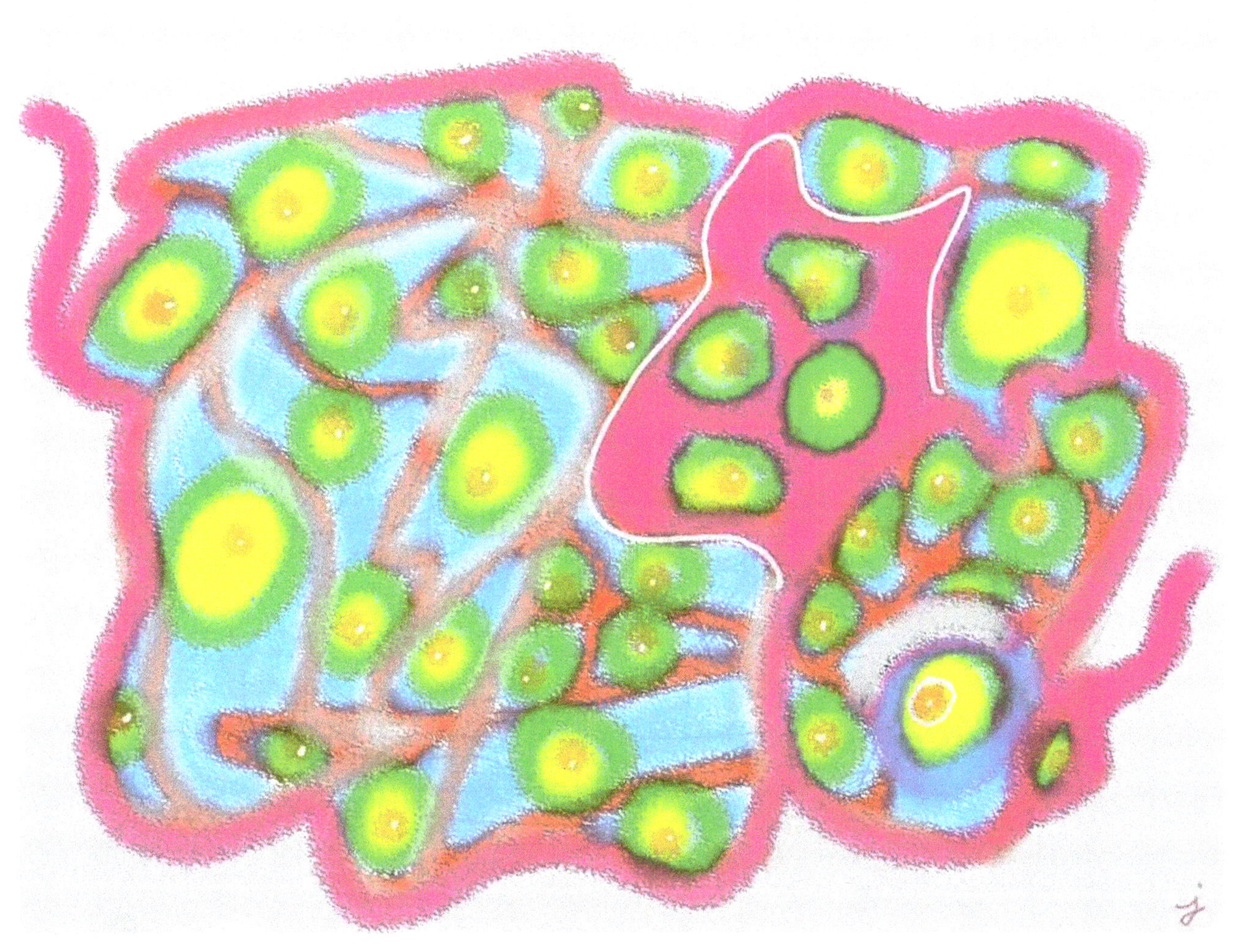

Ollie with the Thousand Eyes

Come with me, go with the flow,
Follow my lead and enjoy the show.
My only purpose on this stage
Is to get you to engage.

I'll make you laugh and warm you up;
I'll tell you jokes and do stand-up.
I'm on a roll and won't relax
Until you've seen all of my acts.

Don't you doubt. I am not feigning;
My ultimate joy is entertaining.
I love to charm and jape and jest,
Make you feel welcome as a guest.

I love to sing, can't wait to dance.
I readily jump at every chance
To shimmy, shake, take you along
Like a conductor wields the baton.

When I become all animated,
You can't but be exhilarated.
I'll drive your excitement to the top.
I'm the master; I'm Emcee Hop!

Emcee Hop

I work terribly hard all day.
   I'm on the ball and don't delay.
I clean and scrub and wash and wipe
Every speck of dirt I swipe.

Making grimy windows shine
With Spic 'n' Span I'm on cloud nine.
I scrub your kitchen smooth and bright
Until it's bathed in lustrous light.

But when the labour of the day
Is done and I collect my pay,
I head home, soak in the tub,
Trim my moustache and go to the pub.

All shout for joy when I arrive;
The joint at once becomes alive.
I order whiskey and vermouth,
I'm *Señor* Suave, Sultan Smooth,

The Lord of Love, Czar of the Bar.
All ladies are on my radar.
I hang out coolly at the counter,
Scanning for my next encounter.

Oh, yes, I draw them in at will.
They're begging me to pay my bill.
Boy, am I good! So very slick
That I can chat up every chick.

When I'm ready to flirt and kiss,
I make a pass and never miss.
It never fails 'cause women trust
That they can squeeze me in their lust!

So I, descendant of the ocean,
Am living in continuous motion.
All babes fall for me and lunge
At me, Clark the Lady-killer Sponge.

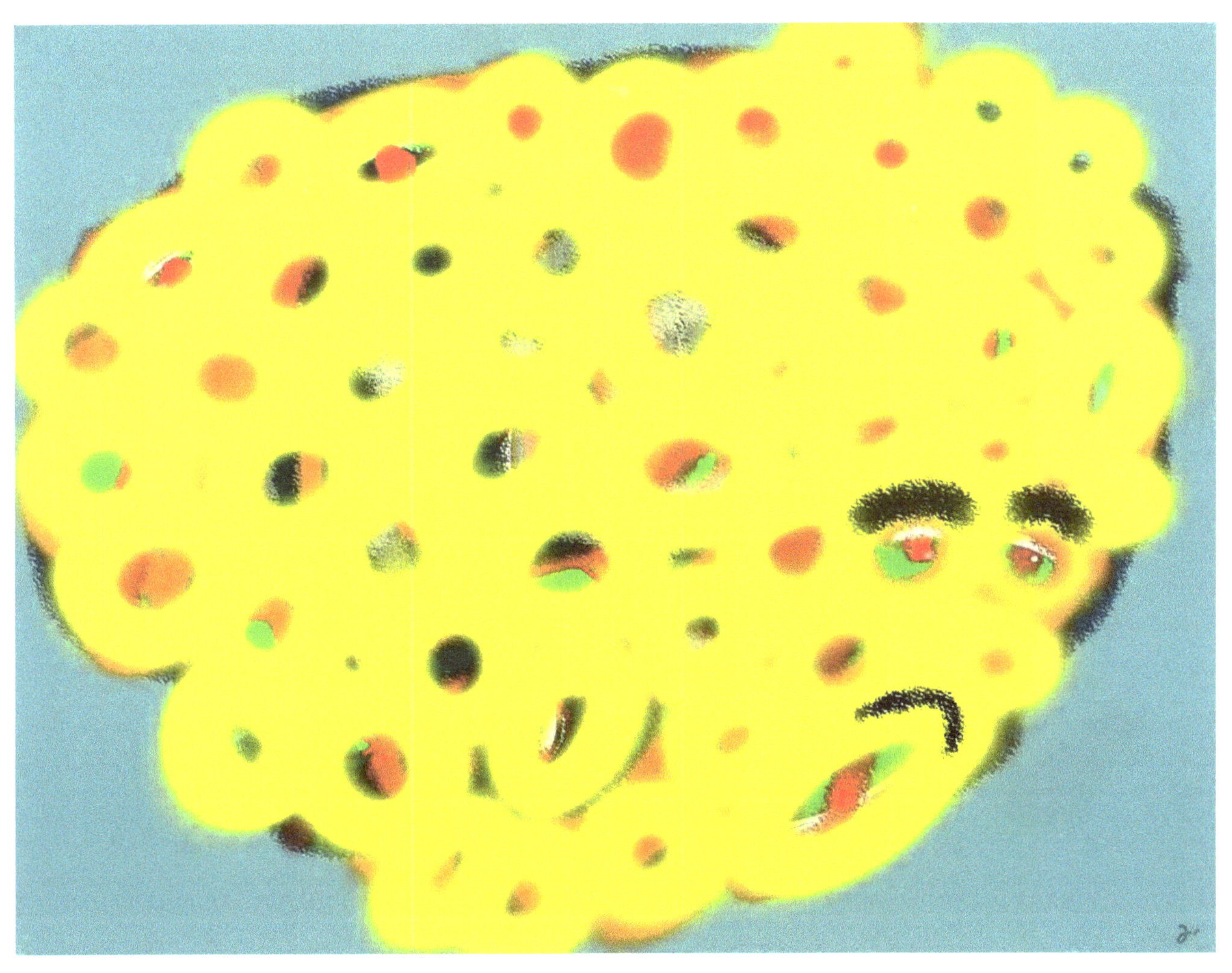

Clark the Lady-killer Sponge

Tired by day, exhausted by night,
I feel like a shadow and look like a fright,
Weary of carrying this weight on my back,
A knight in full armour whose head got a whack.

I'm worn out, depleted and drained,
Barely can move, my muscles are strained.
Yet I have to go on, try to step faster,
Be ultra brave and obey my master.

I want to sleep, I'm tired of this fight;
Haven't eaten for days and would love a bite.
But my Lord does not hear, nor reason he sees.
He's a cranky old man, and his brain is a breeze.

Oh help, oh no, another windmill in sight!
I'm afraid he'll charge and start a fight.
We'll be caught, thrown up in the air,
Then smacked on the ground, it's too much to bear!

I am Rocinante; Don Quixote's my boss.
Please, can you help? Because I'm at a loss;
I want to run, but I almost fall down.
Reader, tell me how to shake off this clown.

What? Is he gone? You mean he's not there?
But I swear that I feel him, as I am a mare!
Maybe he is a phantom only I see,
That merrily tortures me with utter glee!

Do I make it up? Is it my imagination?
Is it just an abject fixation
That I feel and see what has ceased to exist,
A memory of what's long since been dismissed?

I'll call my shrink and find out what's the deal,
If the weight that I feel is fake or real.
Maybe then I can finally stop this strife,
Joyfully be free and get on with my life!

Rocinante

I have four eyes, two on each side.
It is a fact that I can't hide.
And did you know I'm made of carrots
Of all colours, bright as parrots?

So though I may look a little funny,
I'm still an itty-bitty bunny.
I think of me, and simply beam;
I'm my own ultimate dream!

I am Carrot; I'm a rabbit.
Nibbling is my cherished habit.
I chew and gnaw whenever I can.
I am my own most ardent fan!

So I provide my own catering
To feed my ceaseless savouring.
One word of wisdom I'll bequeath:
Never fail to brush your teeth!

Carrot the Rabbit

Where am I? Who put me here?
It seems I'm in a different sphere!
I don't know the real causation
Of this strange hallucination!

Life was peachy, I had fun;
It was a lovely day in the sun.
Made to sing and dance and jive,
I was simply glad to be alive!

Then I saw a lovely weed
With a flower and many a seed.
It looked so tempting, don't know why.
I had to eat it, could not but try!

What happened next I don't remember,
My memory seems a dying ember.
And now I don't know where I am.
It looks like I'm a poor, lost lamb!

Can't fathom where I've landed,
Yet it seems as if I'm stranded
In a space ever so wide,
Thoroughly, intensely purified.

My consciousness is widely expanding,
Yet my legs are barely standing.
I am wrapped in supreme bliss,
The point of which, however, I miss.

My eyes are saucers but where's the cup?
My thoughts are racing, bottled up.
I find that I've begun to weep
For my dear flock of fellow sheep!

I feel forsaken and naïve.
I miss my home; I start to grieve
'Cause Mummy's waiting with the pram;
I hear her calling, 'Lily Lamb?'

Lily Lamb

On time's mirror I do glide,
A mingling of grace and pride,
Profoundly aware of my uniqueness,
Keeper of your silent secrets.

Come to me and trust your fate.
Your worries will soon dissipate;
You will let go of all your fears.
Collect yourself and dry your tears.

I am a swan; Lakey's my name.
I am of supernatural fame.
I will clothe you in gilded light;
Remove the darkness of your night.

I am the ethereal manifestation
Of your greatest transformation.
Through me, you'll see yourself anew,
And to thine own self be true.

Be soft in speech and calm in gaze,
Witness the world in brilliant rays,
And inner beauty you'll behold
In an outer glow of gold.

Lakey the Swan

I'm so big that I have to sit,
And in my clothes, I do not fit.
My tiny legs won't carry my weight,
Must be all the food I ate.

I weigh a lot, don't know how much.
When I walk, I need a crutch,
Or rather two, I have to say,
And in the winter I use a sleigh

To carry me from here to there:
A truly arduous affair,
Involving plenty of assistance
For a long or even quite short distance.

My name is Thea; I'm a turkey.
My every move is a little jerky;
I kind of waggle from left to right,
Holding myself with all my might.

Why this is so, I don't have the answer;
I never dreamed of being a dancer.
In sports, I hardly was a whiz.
It's how things are; it's how life is.

Yet, deep inside, you know, it's true,
I'm feeling somehow strangely blue
Because I know they'll serve me hot,
Straight from a roasting tin or pot.

But I will never lose my hope
So don't expect to see me mope,
And I will challenge my own fate
By trying again to lose some weight!

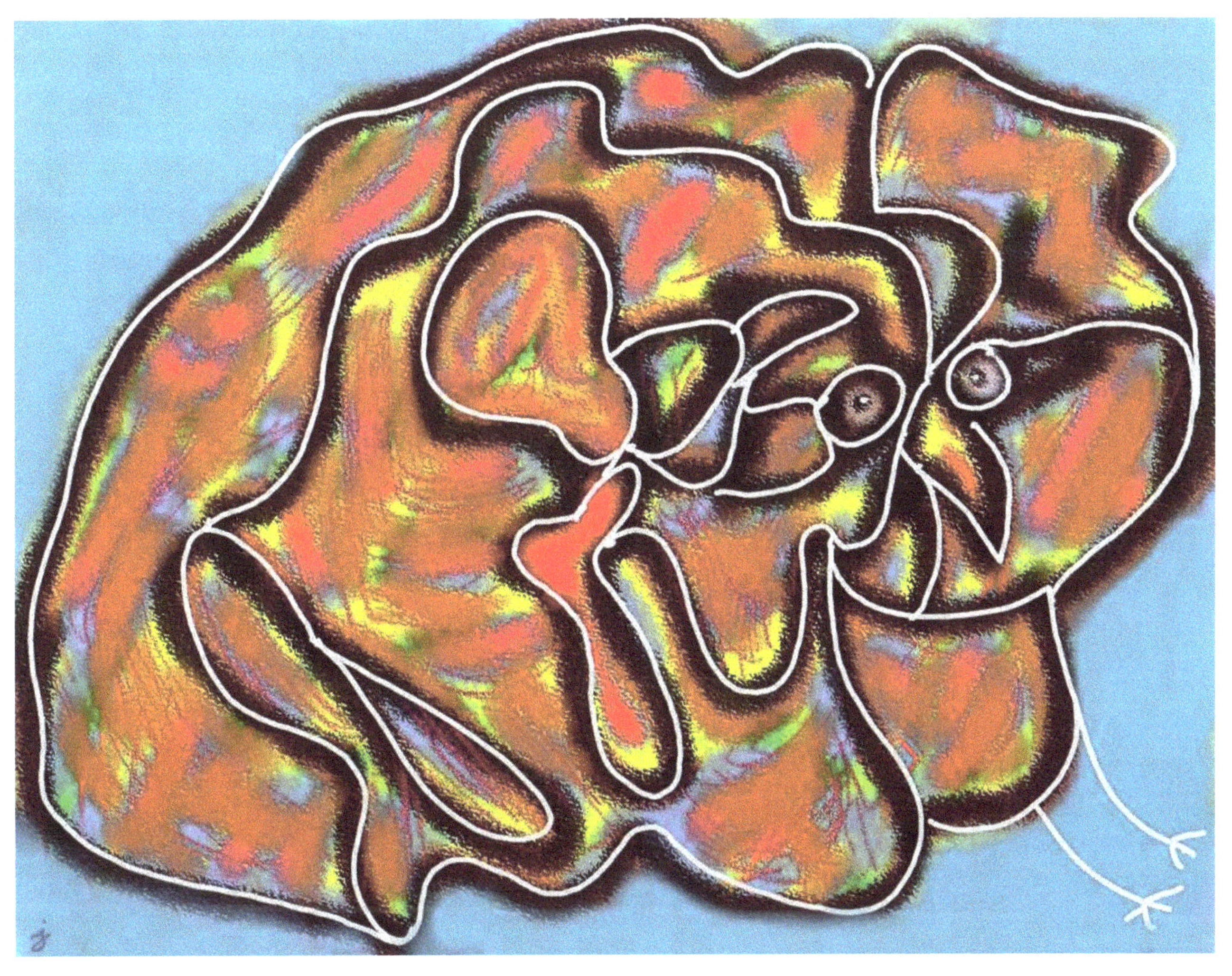

Thea Turkey

I'm cross-eyed; you've seen that right.
My visual aim is a little…light!
Never sure which way I look
At strangers, girls or just a book.

It's the reason I have no friends.
Me as a pal, it makes no sense
'Cause nobody's sure whom I address;
They're at a loss and have to guess.

This constant insularity
Heightens my insecurity.
To me, that is self-evident;
It makes me somehow hesitant.

If it's of interest, my name is Dody.
You'll always see me a little moody,
Melancholic, sullen and glum,
But please don't think that I'm dumb.

I am ready to be your friend,
More than you'll ever comprehend.
I'll stay with you and never leave,
Lie, betray or plain deceive.

I will love you, lick your face,
Be yearning for your warm embrace.
And of my love you'll be so fond
That we'll enjoy an inseparable bond.

Dody Dog

I sing of 'ooh' and 'ah' and 'oh'
With sustained tremolo
Until the audience comes to grips
With my perfectly rounded lips.

I just love to sing on stage,
Melt or swoon or burn with rage.
No song for me can be too sad;
All glum material makes me glad.

I live to feel the misery
Of my heroine's dismal history,
Savour every bit of anguish.
For her lover, I will languish.

I can cry and weep and sob,
Intensely feel the pounding throb
Of my heroine's broken heart
When the lovers' ways do part.

Then I will collapse on cue
When he tearfully bids *adieu,*
And display how I can twitch,
Yet belt out at the highest pitch.

Every night, I look so smitten.
I am Belle the Canto-kitten,
Pouring my all into the role.
To please you is my highest goal!

Belle the Canto-kitten

I am an angel in disguise,
No wings but fly the heavenly skies.
No legs but run to your assistance
When you call from any distance.

I'll comfort you when you're in pain.
When all your efforts have been in vain,
I'll stay with you until you're fine
And your emotions are back in line.

When life's too hard and gets you down,
You sigh too deeply and moan and frown,
When all's a mess, your thoughts are blurred,
Your whole existence seems absurd,

My antennas will pick up your shout;
I'll find the route to you, no doubt.
I'll appear right on command.
And I'm so sunny, you'll be all tanned!

I have no arms, but I can hug,
After all, I'm Oozy the Lovebug.
Without seeming way too sappy,
You'll see that much can make you happy.

I'll ooze with warmth and love and honey,
Make you believe that life is funny,
Build your trust and fill your cup,
And will not leave until you're up!

Oozy the Lovebug

Epilogue

So here we are, in the afterglow.
We really hope you've enjoyed the show.
We've loved to meet you, take this hike
And let you discover what we are like.

Fantabunals we are, far from perfect -
Come to think of it, we all have defects -
But that's how it is; it's who we are,
And we live life fully: sweet, flawed or bizarre.

We've much enjoyed mingling in your mind,
Leaving multiple impressions behind,
Filling your moods with myriad colours,
Unusual shapes, some laughter and wonder.

After our tales you may not be the same,
Play differently in eternal time's game
And enjoy a world as diverse as can be -
Varied it is; on this we agree.

So let's stay together; don't go away.
Let's embrace and continue to play.
Be one with life and hence immerse
In this Fantabulous Universe.

Jan Van Ryckeghem is Belgian. Having always loved stories, he studied history at the University of Ghent and then took off to New York for a life in the theatre. He became versed in method acting and pursued the Master's Programme of the Actor's Studio, also earning a degree in classical acting from the London Academy of Music and Dramatic Art. Currently, he works in the story-telling world of film funding. He loves to draw and compose rhymes. This is his first book.

Continue to play on www.fantabulousuniverse.com